For Elspet and Ruth who look after our pets ~JR

LOOKING AFTER MURPHY
by Jamie Rix and John Bendall-Brunello
British Library Cataloguing in Publication Data
A catalogue record of this book is available from the British Library.
ISBN 0 340 78797 X (HB)
ISBN 0 340 78798 8 (PB)

Text copyright © Jamie Rix 2002
Illustrations copyright © John Bendall-Brunello 2002

The right of Jamie Rix to be identified as the author and
John Bendall-Brunello as the illustrator of this Work
has been asserted by them in accordance with
the Copyright, Designs and Patents Act 1988.

First edition published 2002
10 9 8 7 6 5 4 3 2 1

Published by Hodder Children's Books
a division of Hodder Headline Limited
338 Euston Road London NW1 3BH

Printed in Hong Kong

Looking After Murphy

Written by JAMIE RIX

Illustrated by JOHN BENDALL-BRUNELLO

Hodder
Children's
Books

A division of Hodder Headline Limited

With Granny Lally, it was always difficult to know how much to believe. When Granny Lally said to her grandchildren, Sally and Jim, 'We'll see,' it usually meant, 'We'll ask your father,' which always meant, 'We'll ask your mother'. And if their mother said 'Maybe' that definitely meant 'No!'

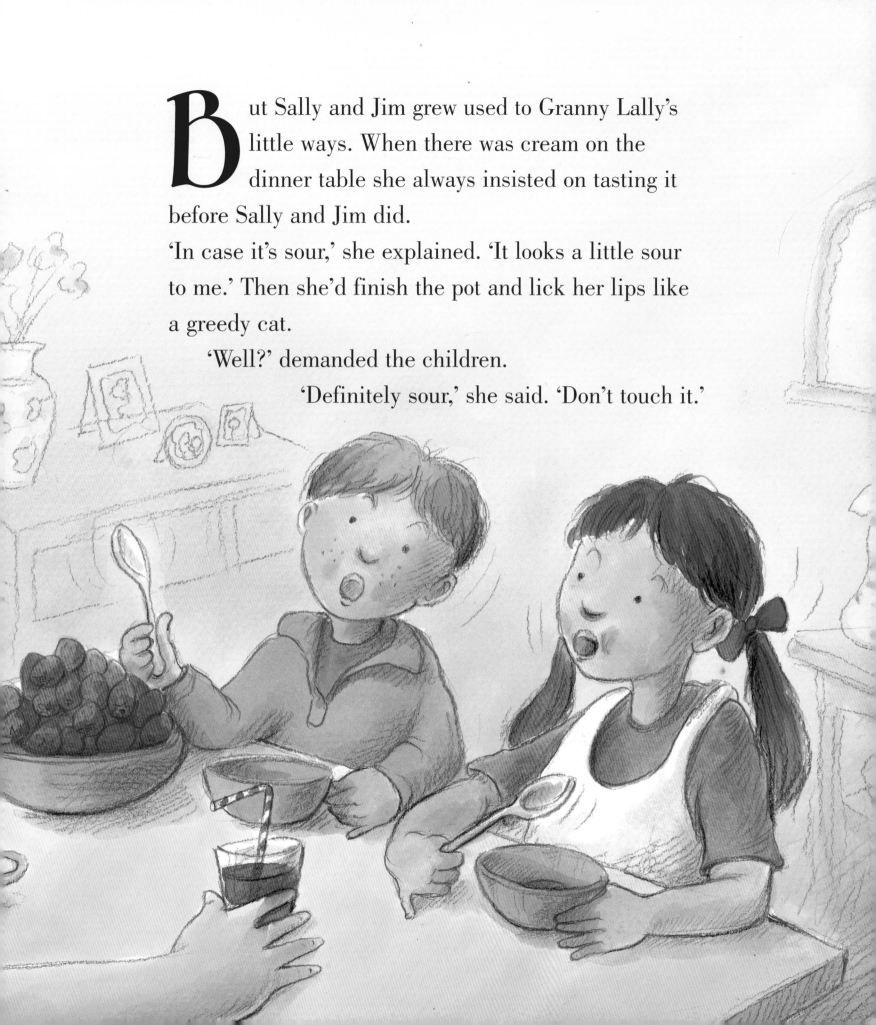

B ut Sally and Jim grew used to Granny Lally's little ways. When there was cream on the dinner table she always insisted on tasting it before Sally and Jim did.

'In case it's sour,' she explained. 'It looks a little sour to me.' Then she'd finish the pot and lick her lips like a greedy cat.

'Well?' demanded the children.

'Definitely sour,' she said. 'Don't touch it.'

She even made Sally and Jim watch her favourite TV programme. 'Doctor's orders,' she explained. 'He said I have to watch an hour of Celebrity Knitting every day.' What could Jim and Sally do? They couldn't call their granny a liar, because grown-ups never lied – especially grannies!

One Christmas, Sally and Jim were given a brown hamster with one white ear and one bent whisker. They called him Murphy and they loved him.

He lived in a big wooden doll's house with shutters on the windows and a lock on the door to keep him out of mischief. Whenever they let Murphy out he always got into trouble.

He burrowed under their duvets, swung from the lampshade and ate their socks.

Before they went away on holiday, Sally and Jim took Murphy to the cottage where Granny Lally lived with her cat. She was looking after Murphy while the children were away.

'Whatever you do, don't let him out of his house unless you're watching him,' said Jim.

'Or he'll run away,' said Sally. 'And you'll never find him.'

Granny Lally laughed. 'I promise I won't take my eyes off Murphy,' she said.

For the next six days Murphy was never out of Granny Lally's sight. They did everything together.

He ran around inside her old jumper while she dug potatoes.

He did back flips in her apron while she cooked pies.

He chewed boiled sweets in her overcoat pocket while she visited the dentist.

ut on the very last night, Granny Lally took her eyes off Murphy. One minute he was sitting on the tap listening to her singing …

... the next, she closed her eyes to hit a top C and
when she opened them again, Murphy was gone.

She leapt out of the bath, wild and wet with worry.
What if the cat had eaten him?

She held the poor thing upside down and gave it a shake, but nothing came out except a slightly startled miaow.

She checked in the fridge in case Murphy was stealing the cheese. She even checked in the broom cupboard in case Murphy had fallen in love with a brush.

But Murphy had vanished.

Granny Lally sat on the stairs and cried.
What an awful grandmother she was! What was
she going to tell her grandchildren – the simple
truth or a whopping great lie?

Early in the morning, she drove to the pet shop and
bought another brown hamster with one white ear and
one bent whisker.

When Sally and Jim arrived Granny Lally crossed
her fingers and lied through her teeth.
'Here's Murphy,' she said. 'He's missed you.'
The hamster didn't even look at the children.

'Why is his whisker bending the wrong way?' asked Sally. 'It was bending down when we left him, but now it's bending up.' 'That's probably because he's so happy to see you again,' lied her grandmother.

'And why has his white ear changed sides?'
puzzled Jim. 'It was on the right when we left him,
but now it's on the left.'
'You're holding him the wrong way round,'
she lied again. The children believed her.
But they couldn't understand why
Murphy didn't love them any more.

T hen, just as they were leaving, another black nose poked out through an upstairs window of the doll's house.

'There's a burglar in Murphy's house!' they yelled.

But when they opened the front door a hamster trotted out. And this one had a whisker that bent down and a white ear on the right. It was the real Murphy. He had been asleep in his bedroom all the time.

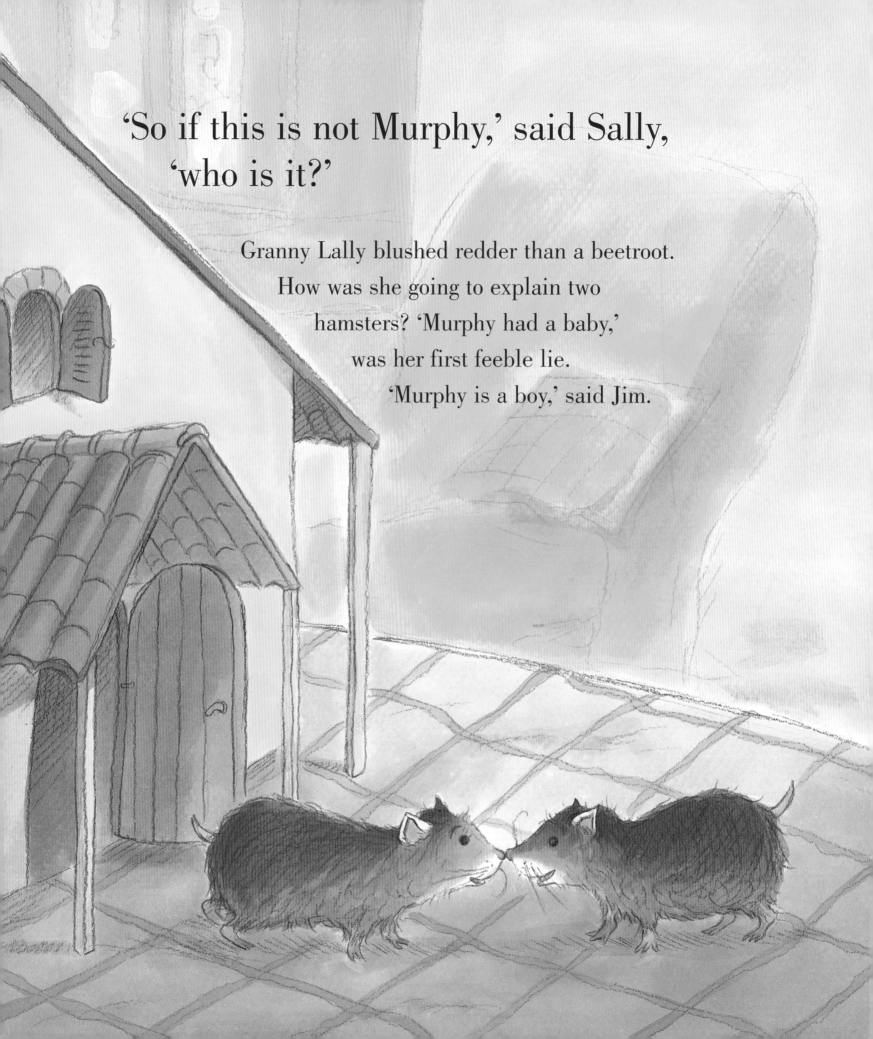

'So if this is not Murphy,' said Sally,
'who is it?'

Granny Lally blushed redder than a beetroot.
How was she going to explain two
hamsters? 'Murphy had a baby,'
was her first feeble lie.
'Murphy is a boy,' said Jim.

'Murphy had a friend round last night for a sleepover,'
was her second feeble lie.
'The doll's house doesn't have a guest room,' said Sally.
'Then it must be Murphy's fiancée,' lied Granny Lally
for the third time.

And because she was their grandmother, and because they were nicely brought up children, and because they respected their elders, Sally and Jim said that they believed her.

Murphy and the fake hamster were married in the
Spring, and when Sally and Jim next went on holiday,
Granny Lally agreed to look after Murphy again.

Only this time, because Murphy was a family man,
she promised to be a little more careful.